D1091204

I'LL TELL YOU A TALE

IAN SERRAILLIER

# I'll Tell You a Tale

*A Collection of Poems
and Ballads*

KESTREL BOOKS

*To Anne and her grandchildren*

*Acknowledgements*

We are grateful to the following for permission to reproduce the photographs:

The Trustees of the British Museum for page 19; Barnaby's Picture Library for pages 29, 40, 58 below, 64, 65; Camera Press for pages 9 (photo by Eric Ray), 16, 27 below (photo by Alfred Gregory), 70 (photo by Tom Weir); John Cleare for page 63; Herts and Essex Observer for page 34; Syndication International for page 74.

The illustrations are by the following artists:
Victor G. Ambrus: page 98; Charles Keeping: pages 86, 89, 100, 107, 111, 113; Hugh Marshall: pages 20, 54, 73, 79, 92, 96; Renate Meyer: pages 68, 77, 85; Mark Peppé: pages 23, 36. The illustration by Victor G. Ambrus first appeared in *Marko's Wedding*, André Deutsch Ltd, 1972, and is reproduced by permission of the publisher.

KESTREL BOOKS
Published by Penguin Books Ltd, Harmondsworth, Middlesex, England

First published as a Longman Structural Reader, 1973
Revised edition published by Kestrel Books 1976
Second impression 1978
Third impression 1982

ISBN 0 7226 5190 2

Filmset by BAS Printers Limited, Wallop, Hampshire
Printed in Hong Kong by Yu Luen Offset Printing Factory Ltd

# CONTENTS

# SECTION ONE

# WALY, WALY

The water is wide, I cannot cross,
And neither have I wings to fly.
Bring me a boat that will carry two,
And we shall row, my love and I.

O down in the meadow the other day,
When gathering flowers bright and gay,
When gathering flowers red and blue,
I little thought what love could do.

I put my hand into a bush,
Thinking the fairest flower to find.
I pricked my finger right to the bone
And left the fairest flower behind.

I leaned my back against an oak,
Thinking it was a trusty tree;
But first it bent and then it broke,
And so did my false love to me.

There is a ship that sails the sea,
She's loaded deep as deep can be,
But not so deep as the love I'm in;
I know not if I sink or swim.

O love is handsome and love is fine,
And love's a jewel while it is new;
But when it is old it's growing cold,
And fades away like morning dew.

# LORD THOMAS AND FAIR ANNET

I

Lord Thomas and Fair Annet
   Sat all day on a hill;
When sun had set and night had come,
   They were talking still.

Lord Thomas said a word in jest
   Fair Annet did not like:
'Unless my friends are pleased with her,
   I'll never marry a wife.'

'If you will never marry a wife,
   No wife will marry you.'
Lord Thomas went to his mother then,
   And knelt upon his knee.

'Tell me, tell me, mother,' he said,
   'O what am I to do?
Shall I take the nut-brown bride
   And let Fair Annet go?'

'The nut-brown bride has land and gold,
   Fair Annet has got none;
The beauty that Fair Annet has,
   O it will soon be gone!'

Lord Thomas went to his sister then:
   'O what am I to do?
Shall I take the nut-brown bride
   And let Fair Annet go?'

'You should take Fair Annet, Thomas,
   And let the brown bride go;
Or one day you may cry, "Alas!
   What's this that I brought home?"'

'No, I'll do as my mother says,
  I'll do as she has planned,
And I will take the nut-brown bride;
  Fair Annet can leave the land.'

2

Fair Annet's father was out of bed
  Before the break of day;
He went at once into the room
  Where Fair Annet lay.

'Get up, get up, Fair Annet,' he said,
  'Put on your silken shoes!
We must go to St Mary's Church,
  The wedding not to miss.'

'My maids, go to my dressing-room,
  And comb my yellow hair.
It shone before, now let it shine
  Twenty times as fair.'

The horse Fair Annet rode upon
  Was easy as the wind;
Shod with silver shoes in front,
  With burning gold behind.

Four-and-twenty silver bells
  Were all tied to its mane;
They tinkled in the northern wind
  Again and yet again.

Four-and-twenty gallant knights
  Rode at Fair Annet's side,
And four-and-twenty ladies fair,
  As if she were a bride.

3

When she came to St Mary's Church,
  She sat down by the door;
And all the people at the wedding
  Turned their heads to stare.

When she walked along the church,
  She shimmered like the sun;
The belt that was around her waist
  With pretty pearls was strung.

She sat down by the nut-brown bride,
  Her eyes they were so clear;
Lord Thomas clean forgot the bride
  When Fair Annet came near.

He had a rose in his hand;
  He gave it kisses three,
And, reaching past the nut-brown bride,
  Laid it on Annet's knee.

Up then spoke the nut-brown bride,
  In jealousy and spite:
'Where did you get the rose-water
  That makes your skin so white?'

'I got all my rose-water
  Where you will find none;
I got all my rose-water
  In my mother's womb.'

The bride she drew a long pin
  From her brown hair,
And struck Fair Annet to the heart;
  Fair Annet spoke no more.

Lord Thomas saw her face turn pale –
    O, what could it be?
But when he saw her dear heart's blood,
    Raging mad was he.

He drew his dagger that was so sharp,
    That was so sharp and neat,
And drove it into the nut-brown bride –
    She fell dead at his feet.

'Now wait for me, Fair Annet, dear,
    Now wait, my dear!' he cried;
Then struck the dagger into his heart,
    And fell dead at her side.

4

They buried him outside the church,
    Where now a birch tree grows;
She lies inside, and from her tomb
    Springs a wild rose.

The tree and rose they grew and grew,
    Longing to be near;
For Lord Thomas and Fair Annet
    They were two lovers dear.

# KISS ME NOW

Kiss me now,
Kiss me cunning,
Kiss me quick,
Mother's coming.

# HAIKU

Alone I cling to
    The freezing mountain and see
        White cloud – below me.

The Haiku is a Japanese form of poetry. In it the poet tries to give the essence of a mood – of something sad, or amusing, or surprising – all within three short lines. The first and third lines should have five syllables and the second line should have seven.

# LORD RANDAL

'O where have you been, Lord Randal, my son?
And where have you been, my handsome young man?'
'I have been to the wood; mother, make my bed soon,
For I'm weary with hunting, and long to lie down.'

'And who did you meet there, Lord Randal, my son?
And who did you meet, my handsome young man?'
'O I met with my true-love; mother, make my bed soon,
For I'm weary with hunting, and long to lie down.'

'And what did she give you, Lord Randal, my son,
And what did she give you, my handsome young man?'
'Eels fried in a pan; mother, make my bed soon,
For I'm weary with hunting, and long to lie down.'

'Who ate what you left, Lord Randal, my son?
Who ate what you left, my handsome young man?'
'My hawks and my hounds; mother, make my bed soon,
For I'm weary with hunting, and long to lie down.'

'And what happened to them, Lord Randal, my son?
And what happened to them, my handsome young man?'
'They stretched out and died; mother, make my bed soon,
For I'm weary with hunting, and long to lie down.'

'O I fear you are poisoned, Lord Randal, my son!
I fear you are poisoned, my handsome young man!'
'O yes, I am poisoned; mother, make my bed soon,
For I'm sick in my heart, and I long to lie down.'

'What d'you leave to your mother, Lord Randal, my son?
What d'you leave to your mother, my handsome young man?'
'Four-and-twenty milk cows; mother, make my bed soon,
For I'm sick in my heart, and I long to lie down.'

'What d'you leave to your sister, Lord Randal, my son?
What d'you leave to your sister, my handsome young
    man?'
'My gold and my silver; mother, make my bed soon,
For I'm sick in my heart, and I long to lie down.'

'What d'you leave to your brother, Lord Randal, my son?
What d'you leave to your brother, my handsome young
    man?'
'My houses and lands; mother, make my bed soon,
For I'm sick in my heart, and I long to lie down.'

'What d'you leave to your true-love, Lord Randal, my
    son?
What d'you leave to your true-love, my handsome young
    man?'
'I leave her hell fire; mother, make my bed soon,
For I'm sick in my heart, and I long to lie down.'

## LIZZIE BORDEN

Lizzie Borden with an axe
Hit her father forty whacks.
When she saw what she had done,
She hit her mother forty-one.

## ROBIN HOOD AND ALAN-A-DALE

Come listen to me, you gallants so free,
    All you that love laughter to hear,
And I will tell you of a bold outlaw
    That lived in Nottinghamshire.

As Robin Hood in the forest stood
    Under the greenwood tree,
He saw a young man in scarlet red
    Singing a roundelay.

As Robin Hood next morning stood
    Among the leaves so gay,
There he saw the same young man
    Come drooping along the way.

The scarlet he wore the day before –
    He'd cast it clean away;
At every step he sighed, 'Alas!
    How wretched I am today!'

Then stepped out brave Little John
    And Much the miller's son;
Which made the young man bend his bow,
    When he saw them come.

'Stand off, stand off,' the young man said.
    'What do you want with me?'
'You must come before our master now,
    Under the greenwood tree.'

When he came before their master,
    Robin asked him courteously,
'O, have you any money to spare
    For my merry men and me?'

'I have no money,' the young man said,
    'But five shillings and a ring.
And that I have kept for seven long years,
    To have at my wedding.

'Yesterday I should have married a girl,
    But she's been taken away
And chosen to be an old knight's delight,
    And my poor heart is slain!'

'What is your name?' said Robin Hood.
    'My name is Alan-a-dale.'
'How much will you pay, if I bring her back
    And give her to you without fail?'

'I have no money,' the young man said,
    'And that is the truth I tell.
But I will swear to be your man
    And ever to serve you well.'

'How many miles to your true-love?
    And tell me no lies, I say.'
'By the faith of my body,' the young man said,
    'She lives five miles away.'

Then Robin hastened over the fields,
    He didn't linger or wait,
Till he came to the church where the wedding was
    And rushed in through the gate.

'What's this? What's this?' the bishop said.
    'Now tell the truth to me.'
'I'm a bold harper,' said Robin Hood,
    'The best in the north country.'

'O welcome, O welcome,' the bishop said.
    'That music pleases me.'
'You'll have no music,' said Robin Hood,
    'Till the bride and the bridegroom I see.'

Just then a wealthy knight came in,
    Who was both grave and old,
And after him a dainty lass,
    Who shone like glittering gold.

'This is no fit match,' said Robin,
    'That you are making here;
And now that we have come to the church,
    The bride shall choose her own dear.'

Then Robin put his horn to his mouth
    And blew blasts two or three;
And four-and-twenty bowmen brave
    Came leaping over the lea.

And when they came to the churchyard,
    Marching all in a row,
The first man was Alan-a-dale
    To give bold Robin his bow.

'This is your true-love,' Robin said,
    'Young Alan, as I hear say;
And you shall be married this very hour,
    Before we depart away.'

'That shall not be,' the bishop said,
    'For *your* word shall not stand.
They must be asked three times in church –
    That's the law of our land.'

Robin pulled off the bishop's coat
    And put it on Little John.
'By the faith of my body,' Robin said,
    'The clothing makes the man.'

When Little John went into the choir,
    The people began to laugh;
He asked them seven times in the church
    Lest three times wasn't enough.

'Who's giving the bride?' said Little John.
    'I am.' Up Robin stood.
'The man who takes her from Alan-a-dale
    Must reckon with Robin Hood.'

And so the wedding came to an end –
    The bride looked fresh as a queen;
And then they returned to the merry green wood
    Among the leaves so green.

# RIDDLES

1

Cut me, and I'll make you cry;
Cook me, and your tears will dry.

2

I look at you
And you at me,
But are you really there?
For when I step
To right or left,
You are not anywhere.

3

White or grey,
The mountains wear it;
You can't patch
Or stitch or tear it.

# THE RESCUE

The wind is loud,
The wind is blowing,
The waves are big,
The waves are growing.
What's that? What's that?
A dog is crying,
It's in the sea,
A dog is crying.
His or hers
Or yours or mine?
A dog is crying,
A dog is crying.

Is no one there?
A boat is going,
The waves are big,
A man is rowing,
The waves are big,
The waves are growing.
Where's the dog?
It isn't crying.
His or hers
Or yours or mine?
Is it dying?
Is it dying?

The wind is loud,
The wind is blowing,
The waves are big,
The waves are growing.
Where's the boat?
It's upside down.
And where's the dog,

And must it drown?
His or hers
Or yours or mine?
O, must it drown?
O, must it drown?

Where's the man?
He's on the sand,
So tired and wet
He cannot stand.
And where's the dog?
It's in his hand,
He lays it down
Upon the sand.
His or hers
Or yours or mine?
The dog is mine,
The dog is mine!

So tired and wet
And still it lies.
I stroke its head,
It opens its eyes,
It wags its tail,
So tired and wet.
I call its name,
For it's my pet,
Not his or hers
Or yours, but mine –
And up it gets,
And up it gets!

# THE HANGMAN'S TREE

'Hangman, hangman, hold your hand,
  O hold it just a while!
For there I see my father coming,
  Riding many a mile.

'Father, have you brought me gold?
  Will you set me free?
Or have you come to see me hung
  From the hangman's tree?'

'No, I haven't brought you gold,
  I will not set you free,
But I have come to see you hung
  From the hangman's tree.'

'Hangman, hangman, hold your hand,
  O hold it just a while!
For there I see my mother coming,
  Riding many a mile.

'Mother, have you brought me gold?
  Will you set me free?
Or have you come to see me hung
  From the hangman's tree?'

'No, I haven't brought you gold,
  I will not set you free,
But I have come to see you hung
  From the hangman's tree.'

'Hangman, hangman, hold your hand,
  O hold it just a while!
For there I see my sister coming,
  Riding many a mile.

'Sister, have you brought me gold?
    Will you set me free?
Or have you come to see me hung
    From the hangman's tree?'

'No, I haven't brought you gold,
    I will not set you free,
But I have come to see you hung
    From the hangman's tree.'

'Hangman, hangman, hold your hand,
    O hold it just a while!
For there I see my sweetheart coming,
    Riding many a mile.

'Sweetheart, have you brought me gold?
    Will you set me free?
Or have you come to see me hung
    From the hangman's tree?'

'Yes, O yes, I've brought you gold,
    I will set you free,
For I have come to take you down
    From the hangman's tree.'

# AS I WAS COMING DOWN THE STAIR

As I was coming down the stair,
I met a man who wasn't there.
He wasn't there again today:
I *wish* that man would go away!

DIVERS BEFORE DRIVERS
DONT BE A FOOL
SAVE OUR SWIMMING PO
DONT FORGET
TOWN POOL

# NO SWIMMING IN THE TOWN

The swimming pool is closed –
There isn't any money.
What shall we do?
It isn't very funny.

We'll open up the school
And chase away the porter,
Turn on the taps
And fill it up with water.


# THE GOLDEN VANITY

A ship called *The Golden Vanity*
Saw a Turkish man-of-war at sea.

The ship-boy spoke. 'Captain,' said he,
'If I sink her, what will you give to me?'

The captain replied, 'You're brave and bold.
I'll give you a box of silver and gold.'

'Then tie me tight in a black bull's skin,
And throw me in the sea, to sink or swim!'

They tied him tight in a black bull's skin
And threw him in the sea, to sink or swim.

The water was cold, but he kept afloat,
And away he swam to the Turkish boat.

Some were playing cards and some throwing dice,
When he made three holes in the boat with his knife.

He made three more . . . Then – lose or win –
What did it matter when the sea rushed in?

Some cut their coats, some cut their caps
To try to stop the salt water gaps.

About and about and about swam he,
And back to *The Golden Vanity*.

'Now throw me a rope and pull me on board!
Captain, see that you keep your word!'

'I'll throw you no rope,' the captain cried.
'Goodbye. I leave you to drift with the tide.'

Out spoke the ship-boy, out spoke he,
'What if I sink you? How would that be?'

'Throw him a rope!' the sailors cried.
They threw him a rope – but on deck he died.

The black bull-skin: the ship-boy probably used it to disguise himself as
a dolphin.

# LIMERICKS

There was a young lady of Spain,
Who couldn't go out in the rain,
  For she'd lent her umbrella
  To Queen Isabella,
Who never returned it again.

There was an old lady who said,
When she found a thief under her bed,
  'Get up from the floor;
  You're too close to the door,
And I fear you'll catch cold in the head.'

There was a young fellow of Perth,
Who was born on the day of his birth;
  He was married, they say,
  On his wife's wedding day,
And he died when he quitted the earth.

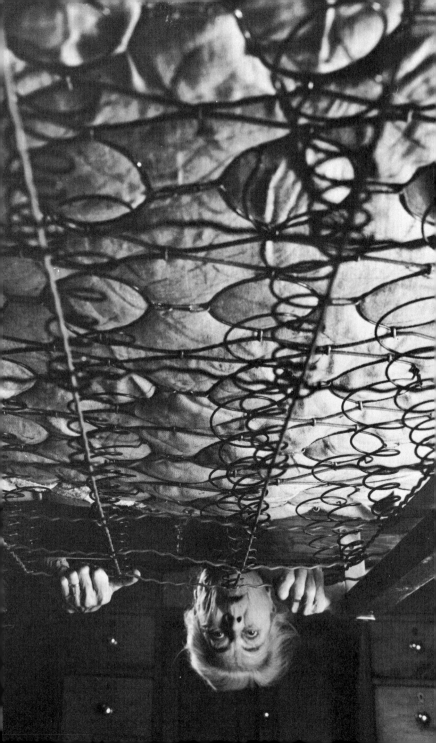

# JACK

'I'm sad. I want to die,' said Jack,
And laid his head on the railway track.
A train was coming down the line –
He pulled his head back just in time.

# SECTION TWO

# YOUNG HUNTING

The lady stood at her castle door,
    At her castle door she stood;
She thought she heard a bridle ring;
    And O that sound was good!

She thought it was her father dear
    Riding over the sand;
But it was Young Hunting, her true-love,
    Hastening to her hand.

'You're welcome, welcome, Young Hunting,
    To coal and candle-light.
You're welcome, welcome, Young Hunting,
    To sleep in my room tonight.'

'I thank you for your coal, madam,
    And for your candles too;
But a fairer girl at Clyde Water
    I love better than you.'

'A fairer girl than me, Young Hunting?
    A fairer girl than me?
A fairer girl than ten of me
    You surely never did see?'

He leaned down from his saddle then
    To give her a kiss so sweet.
She plunged a penknife into his heart,
    And O, the wound was deep!

'O hide this deed, my serving girl!
    O hide this deed, be true;
And all my silken Christmas clothes
    At Easter shall be for you.'

They sat Young Hunting on his horse
   The way he used to ride,
With a hunting horn around his neck
   And a sharp sword at his side.

Away they rode to Clyde Water,
   And there they threw him in;
They laid a green turf on his chest
   To hold the good lord down.

'Lie there, lie there, Young Hunting!
   Your bed is dark and deep.
The girl you loved at Clyde Water
   Will long for you and weep.'

Up and spoke a wily bird
   As it watched from a tree on high:
'Young Hunting had no love but you;
   An ill death may you die!'

'Come down, come down, my pretty bird,
   And pick the wheat from my hand.
I'll give you a cage of beaten gold,
   Set on a silver stand.'

'I won't come down, I shan't come down,
   To such a traitor as you;
You'd twist my head from my neck-bone,
   And fling it into the sea.'

The King went to the lady's castle.
   'Where is my son?' he cried.
'Young Hunting he shall ride with me
   And gallop at my side.'

She turned to the right and round about,
    She swore by the golden corn,
'I have not seen Young Hunting, sir,
    Since yesterday at morn.'

She turned to the right and round about,
    She swore by the silver moon,
'I have not seen Young Hunting, sir,
    Since yesterday at noon.

'I fear he's lost in Clyde Water,
    I fear your son is drowned.'
The King sent for his diving men –
    Young Hunting was not found.

Up and spoke the wily bird:
    'You must look for him by night.
Over the place Young Hunting lies,
    The candles will burn bright.'

They looked no more for him by day,
    They looked for him by night;
And over the place Young Hunting lay
    Were candles burning bright.

The first grip his mother got
    Was of his yellow hair;
Sad, O sad it was for her
    To see his body there.

The next grip his mother got
    Was of his milk-white hand;
Sad, O sad it was for her
    To bring him so far to land.

White, white were the wounds they washed,
    Cold, and waxen white;
But when the traitor stood before them,
    The blood came springing bright.

The King sent his men to the wood
    To cut down thorn and fern
And build a great bonfire there,
    That false lady to burn.
'I never killed him,' the lady cried.
    'It was my serving girl.'

No fire would touch the serving girl,
    Neither on cheek or chin;
But it took fast on those two hands
    That threw Young Hunting in;
It took on all her body fair
    And healed the deadly sin.

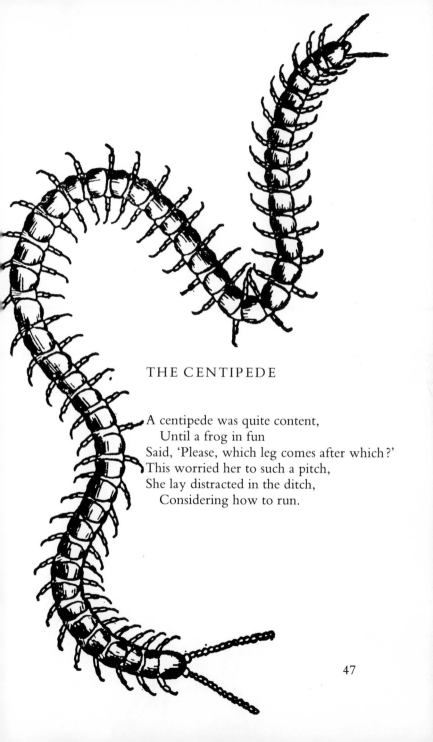

## THE CENTIPEDE

A centipede was quite content,
    Until a frog in fun
Said, 'Please, which leg comes after which?'
This worried her to such a pitch,
She lay distracted in the ditch,
    Considering how to run.

47

## SPELLS

*To be said to a balloon being blown up*

Love me, you'll grow fat and fly,
Hate me, you'll grow thin and die.
Sail, O sail the windy sky!
    Hate me, thinner,
    Nothing for dinner;
    Love me, fatter,
    Butter and batter.
Fatter, fatter, fatter, fatter –

BANG

*To get rid of the 'flu*

First day – freeze and bake;
Second day – shiver and shake;
Third day – 'flu, fly!
But if you sit in the snow you'll die.

*To find a lost season ticket*

Stay, if fallen on the floor;
Flap, if hidden behind a door;
Jump, if in some guilty pocket;
Hear me, hear me,
Season ticket!
If I sing the spell in vain,
I cannot come to school again.

50

# LITTLE MUSGRAVE

The people went to church one day
   To join their priest in prayer;
But Little Musgrave went to church
   To see the ladies there.

One was tall and dressed in green,
   Another dark and small;
Then Lord Barnard's wife came in,
   The fairest of them all.

She cast an eye on Little Musgrave
   Bright as summer sun;
And Little Musgrave thought to himself,
   This lady's heart I've won.

'I've loved you, Little Musgrave,'
   She said, 'for many a day.'
'And I have loved you too, fair lady,
   But never dared to say.'

'I have a room at Mulberry,
   And it is dainty and bright.
Go there, Little Musgrave, go,
   And lie in my arms tonight.'

Her little page-boy heard her speak,
   As by her coach he ran:
'Though I'm her page, I'll tell my lord,
   For I'm Lord Barnard's man.'

'O little page,' Lord Barnard said,
   'If what you say is true,
All my land in Mulberry
   I shall give to you.

'But if you're lying, little page,
    In what you say to me,
If you're lying you shall hang
    Upon the highest tree.'

He called up all his merry men:
    'Come bring my horse to me,
For at Mulberry tonight
    I must surely be.'

'What's that I hear?' said Little Musgrave,
    As in her bed he lay.
'I think it is Lord Barnard's horn,
    "Away, Musgrave, away!" '

'Lie still, lie still, Little Musgrave,
    Keep me from the cold.
It's nothing but a shepherd boy
    Driving sheep to the fold.

'Your falcon's sitting on its perch,
    Your horse has oats and hay,
And you have a lady in your arms, –
    Why must you go away?'

Lord Barnard came to Mulberry
    And leapt down from his horse;
He plucked out three silver keys
    And opened all the doors.

He lifted up the coverlet,
    He lifted up the sheet:
'How now, how now, Little Musgrave,
    D'you find my lady sweet?'

'I find her sweet,' said Little Musgrave,
    'But sweetness turns to fear;
I'd give three hundred pounds to be
    Anywhere but here.'

'Get out of bed, put on your clothes!
    Get up!' Lord Barnard said.
'I will not have it told of me
    I killed a man in bed.

'I have two jewelled swords that cost
    A fortune from my purse.
You shall have the best of them,
    And I shall have the worse.'

The first stroke Little Musgrave struck,
    He hurt Lord Barnard sore;
The next stroke Lord Barnard struck,
    Musgrave could strike no more.

Then fair Lady Barnard spoke,
    As still she lay in bed:
'I'll pray for you, Little Musgrave,
    Though you now are dead.

'And I will wish your soul well,
    As long as I have life.
I will not pray for you, Barnard,
    Though I'm your wedded wife.'

He took his sword and killed her then.
    Great pity it was to see
The red drops of the lady's blood
    Run trickling down her knee!

'Shame on you, my merry men!
   You should have held me back;
You should have struck the sword from my hand,
   For I was raging mad!

'I've killed the bravest knight that ever
   Galloped on the green.
I've killed the fairest lady
   That man has ever seen.

'A grave, a grave!' Lord Barnard cried.
   'Bury them in the earth;
But lay her head on his right hand, –
   She was of nobler birth.

'Then darken all my windows
   With shutters all about;
There is not a living man
   Will see me now walk out.

'Put away my fine clothes,
   My silver brush and comb;
Let burning coal and candle-light
   Never shine at home.

'I've killed the bravest knight that ever
   Galloped on the green.
I've killed the fairest lady
   That man has ever seen.'

# PRISONER AND JUDGE

1

The prisoner was walking round and round the prison
    yard.
He had a low forehead and cruel eyes;
You couldn't trust him anywhere.

He dressed up as a judge; he put on a wig and robes
And sat in court in the judge's place.
And everyone said:
    'What a deep forehead he has, what learned eyes!
    How wise he looks!
    You could trust him anywhere.'

2

The judge was sitting in court in the judge's plaçe.
He had a deep forehead and learned eyes;
You could trust him anywhere.

He dressed up as a prisoner; he put on prisoner's clothes
And walked round and round the prison yard.
And everyone said:
    'What a low forehead he has, what cruel eyes!
    How stupid he looks!
    You couldn't trust him anywhere.'

# RIDDLES

What a hideous cackling and whistling
Interrupt my sleep!
I open the curtains. What do I see and hear? . . .
Two brooms brushing the tree-tops,
Two cloaks blowing in the wind,
Two cats holding tight,
Two jockeys shouting,
'I'll beat you to the moon! I'll beat you to the moon!'

I wonder *which* will win.


2

These golden waves bow to the rule of the wind –
    He wears the crown –
Till a red ship comes loudly through the sea
    And cuts them down.

## MAY COLVIN

False Sir John with fiery heart
  To court his lady came;
She was her father's only heir,
  May Colvin was her name.

He courted her in bower and hall,
  He wooed her every day,
Until at last he'd wrung consent
  To mount and ride away.

'Go fetch me some of your father's gold
  And of your mother's too;
I'll take you to a northern land,
  And there I'll marry you.'

She went to her father's treasure chest,
  Where all his money was kept;
She took the gold and left the silver
  While he soundly slept.

Then she went to her father's stables,
  Undid the bolted door;
Twelve horses, white and dapple-grey
  Stood champing on the floor.

She mounted on a milk-white horse,
  He chose a dapple-grey;
And only her parrot in his cage
  Saw them ride away.

They came at last to a lonely cliff
  Washed by the waves, and high;
The rocks below were steep and sharp,
  And none could hear her cry.

'Get off your horse,' cried false Sir John,
  'And see your bridal bed.
Seven wives I've thrown to the waves,
  And you'll be the eighth,' he said.

'Take off, take off your shining jewels,
  So costly and so brave;
For they're too precious and too fine
  To throw in the salt sea wave.

'Take off, take off your silken dress,
  Your stockings and satin shoes,
Take off your gloves, your coat and vest –
  They are too good to lose.'

'Then turn your back on me, false Sir John,
  Look at the leaves of the tree.
It is not right for a gentleman
  A naked woman to see.'

Loud he laughed, as he turned his back
  To look at the leaves of the tree;
She twined her arms about his waist
  And threw him into the sea.

'O, reach me your hand!' cried false Sir John.
  'O, help me – I shall drown!
I'll take you home to your father's house
  And safely set you down.'

'You'll get no help from me, Sir John,
  No help at all,' said she.
'You could not lie in a colder bed
  Than the one you meant for me.'

She mounted on her milk-white horse
  And led the dapple-grey;
She rode till she came to her father's house
  Before the break of day.

Up and spoke her pretty parrot,
  'May Colvin, where have you been?
And what has become of false Sir John?
  With *you* he last was seen.'

'O, hold your tongue, my pretty parrot!
  Tell no tales of me;
And your cage shall be made of beaten gold
  And the bars of ivory.'

Her father was lying asleep in bed.
  He woke with an angry yawn:
'What is the matter, you prattling parrot?
  There are still two hours till dawn.'

'The cat was scratching the door of my cage,
  Tormenting me, I say.
I was calling out to May Colvin
  To chase the cat away.'

# THE TWO RAVENS

As I was walking all alone,
I heard two ravens cry and moan;
I heard the one to the other say,
'Where shall we go and dine today?'

'In the ditch below the field
There lies a knight that's newly killed;
And nobody knows that he lies there
But his hawk, his hound, and his lady fair.

'His hound has gone to hunt the deer,
His hawk has flown to the empty air,
His lady's found another man;
So we'll have dinner while we can.

'His white neck-bone will be your prize,
And I'll pick out his two blue eyes;
With one lock of his golden hair
We'll line our nest, when it is bare.

'Many a man for him will mourn,
But none shall know where he has gone;
Over his bones, when they are bare,
The wind shall blow for evermore.'

## WEEPING WILLOW IN
## MY GARDEN

My willow's like a frozen hill
Of green waves, when the wind is still;
But when it blows, the waves unfreeze
And make a waterfall of leaves.

# NOT SIXTEEN

I wasn't sixteen when I left school.
My parents called me a pig-headed fool;
They told me to listen to what they said,
But I married a boy in the timber trade.

He lost his job when they shut the mill;
He didn't care and I loved him still;
We had good weather and friends to thank
That we both kept well and ate and drank.

There's a baby coming; we live in a tent,
As there isn't a house or room to rent.
Now winter's upon us, what shall we do
When the wind blows and the rain comes through?

## THE GREAT SEAL

A mother sat with her baby son;
    'By-loo, my baby,' she sang to him.
'I wonder, where is your father now?
    Is it land or sea that he lives in?'

A shape rose out of the darkness then
    And stood beside the mother's bed.
'Here I am, the baby's father,
    Though I look rough and fierce,' he said.

'I am a man when on the land,
    And I am a seal when in the sea;
And when I'm far away from land,
    I live in the waves of Shul Skerrie.'

Then he took out a purse of gold
    And put it on the mother's knee.
'Keep the purse of gold,' he said,
    'And give my baby son to me.

'And it shall happen, one summer's day,
    When the sun shines hot on every stone,
That I will take my little son
    And teach him how to swim alone.

'And you shall marry a proud gunner,
    And a proud gunner I'm sure he'll be;
And the first shot he ever fires,
    He'll shoot my baby son and me.'


THE FALSE KNIGHT UPON
THE ROAD

'O where are you going?'
    *Said the false knight on the road.*
'I'm going to school,'
    *Said the small boy, and still he stood.*

'What's that on your back?'
    *Said the false knight on the road.*
'My books, can't you see?'
    *Said the small boy, and still he stood.*

'What's that under your arm?'
  *Said the false knight on the road.*
'Coal for the school fire, can't you see?'
  *Said the small boy, and still he stood.*

'Who owns those sheep?'
  *Said the false knight on the road.*
'They're mine and my mother's,'
  *Said the small boy, and still he stood.*

'How many of them are mine?'
  *Said the false knight on the road.*
'All those with blue tails,'
  *Said the small boy, and still he stood.*

'I wish you were on that tree over there,'
  *Said the false knight on the road.*
'And a good ladder under me,'
  *Said the small boy, and still he stood.*

'And the ladder would break,'
  *Said the false knight on the road.*
'And you'd fall down,'
  *Said the small boy, and still he stood.*

'I wish you were in the sea,'
  *Said the false knight on the road.*
'And a good ship under me,'
  *Said the small boy, and still he stood.*

'And the ship would break,'
  *Said the false knight on the road.*
'And *you* be drowned,'
  *Said the small boy, and still he stood.*

For acting and speaking. The false knight is the devil in disguise. He is
trying to terrify the small boy so that he can carry him off. The boy
refuses to be terrified and answers his questions cheekily, going one
better than the devil each time. The devil can see very well that the
small bag of coal is on the boy's back, and the satchel of books under his
arm; but the boy makes out that it's the other way round. The sheep
really belong to the knight. 'Those with blue tails': there was no blue
dye in the Middle Ages. Shepherds used red dye for marking sheep. At
the end the knight loses his temper, and the boy escapes.

73

# FISH IN A POLLUTED RIVER

His mother's dead. And now his aunt
Says, 'Where's the purifying plant?
He cannot breathe, he cannot swim,
Because of what you've done to him.'

# THE GARDENER

The gardener stood at the garden gate,
   A primrose in his hand;
He saw a lovely girl come by,
   Slim as a willow wand.

'O lady, can you fancy me,
   And will you share my life?
All my garden flowers are yours,
   If you will be my wife.

'The white lily will be your shirt,
   It suits your body best;
With cornflowers in your hair,
   A red rose on your breast.

'Your gloves will be the marigold,
   Glittering on your hand;
Your dress will be the sweet-william
   That grows upon the bank.'

'Young man, I cannot be your wife;
    I fear it will not do.
Although you care for me,' she said,
    'I cannot care for you.

'As you've provided clothes for me
    Among the summer flowers,
So I'll provide some clothes for you
    Among the winter showers.

'The fallen snow will be your shirt,
    It suits your body best;
Your head will be wound with the eastern wind,
    With the cold rain on your breast.

'Your boots will be of the seaweed
    That drifts upon the tide;
Your horse will be the white wave –
    Leap on, young man, and ride!'

.

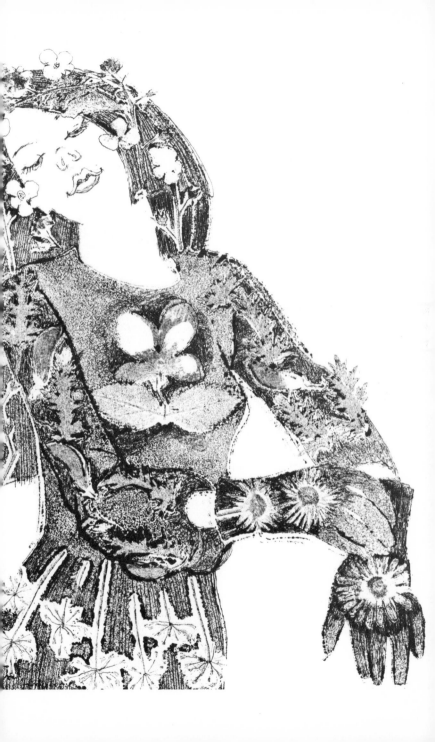

# THE WILL

There was an old man who had three sons
And seventeen horses. 'I've written my will,'
He told his sons. 'I'm going to leave
My horses to the three of you.
But you must share them as I say.'

The old man died. The will was opened:
'To my three sons I leave
My seventeen horses.
My eldest son shall take half;
My second son shall take a third;
My youngest son shall take a ninth.
   *Shed no blood,*
   *Do not kill;*
   *You must obey*
   *Your father's will.'*

The three sons were puzzled. At school
They'd been well taught, but not so well
That they could divide
   17 by 2,
            17 by 3,
                     17 by 9,
And still obey their father's will.

What did they do?

They went to a wise man and asked
His advice. 'I will give you a horse,'
Said the wise man. 'Now go away
And obey your father's will.'

They took the horse and went away.

They now had eighteen horses.
The eldest son took half;
The second son took a third;
The youngest son took a ninth.
And the wise man's horse? They gave it back.

Why did the old man write his will like that?

# LOUDSPEAKER SONG FOR A SUPERMARKET

The plastic flowers shout, 'Hello!
From washing powder packs we grow.
No sun, no rain, we catch the dust
And never die. This buy's a MUST!'

# SECTION THREE

# THE UNQUIET GRAVE

The wind is blowing today, my love,
    And a few small drops of rain;
I never had more than one true-love –
    In the cold grave she was lain.

I'll do as much for my true-love
    As any young man may;
I'll sit and mourn beside her grave
    For twelve months and a day.

When twelve months and a day were up,
    The dead began to speak:
'O who sits weeping on my grave
    And will not let me sleep?'

' 'Tis I, my love, sits on your grave
    And will not let you sleep;
I ask for one kiss of your clay-cold lips,
    And that is all I seek.'

'You ask for one kiss of my clay-cold lips;
    But my breath smells earthy strong;
If you have one kiss of my clay-cold lips,
    Your time will not be long.

' 'Tis down in the green garden,
    Love, where we used to walk;
The finest flower that ever was seen
    Is withered to a stalk.

People used to believe that too much weeping for the dead prevented
them from resting.

'The stalk is withered dry, my love,
   So will our hearts decay;
So make yourself content, my love,
   Till God calls you away.'

# JEALOUSY

'Who lived in the empty house,
    Behind that door?'
'A widow, and her son
    Back from the war.'

'What did he bring with him?
    Did he come alone?'
'He brought his girl; his mother
    Sent her home.'

'He took her away? From the jealous
    House he fled?'
'He stayed, was ill; five years
    He lay in bed.'

'Who came to visit him?
    Who crossed the floor?'
'Except his mother, no-
    body he saw –
        No doctor,
        Nurse,
        Priest,
        Man,
        Woman,
        Or child;
For if they came, his mother
    Stood in the door.'

'What of the girl? Was there nothing
    She could do?'
'She told their story, and tells it
    Now to you.'

# THE HEADLESS GARDENER

A gardener, Tobias Baird,
Sent his head to be repaired;
He thought, as nothing much was wrong,
He wouldn't be without it long.

Ten years he's weeded path and plot,
A headless gardener, God wot,
Always hoping (hope is vain)
To see his noddle back again.

Don't pity him for his distress –
He never sent up his address.


# SWEET WILLIAM'S GHOST

There came a ghost to Margaret's door,
   With many a grievous groan;
He knocked and knocked upon the door –
   But answer made she none.

'Is that my father Philip,
   Or is it my brother John?
Or is it my true-love Willy,
   From Scotland now come home?'

'It's not your father Philip,
    It's not your brother John;
But it's your true-love Willy,
    From Scotland now come home.

'Sweet Margaret, dear Margaret,
    Speak to me, O speak!
I promised you I'd give my love –
    O give my promise back!'

'That promise you will never get,
    That gift you'll never win,
Until you come inside my house
    And kiss my cheek and chin.'

'If I come inside your house,
    I am no earthly man;
If I kiss your rosy lips,
    Your days will not be long.

'Sweet Margaret, dear Margaret,
    Speak to me, O speak!
I promised you I'd give my love –
    O give my promise back!'

'That promise you will never get,
    That gift you'll never win,
Until you take me to the church
    And wed me with a ring.'

'My bones are in the churchyard
    Beside the lonely sea.
It is my spirit, Margaret, speaking –
    Listen, love, to me.'

She stretched out her lily-white hand
    And laid it on his breast:
'I give your promise back, Willy –
    Dear spirit, be at rest.'

She tucked up her green dress
    Below her knee and ran;
All the long winter night
    She followed the dead man.

'Is there any room at your head, Willy?
    Or any room at your feet?
Or any room at your side, Willy,
    Where I may softly creep?'

'There's no room at my head, Margaret,
    There's no room at my feet;
There's no room at my side, Margaret;
    My coffin's made too neat.'

Then up and crowed the red red cock
    And up and crowed the grey.
'It's time, it's time, dear Margaret,
    That you were going away.'

No more the ghost spoke to her,
    But with a grievous groan,
He vanished in a cloud of mist
    And left her all alone.

'O stay, my only true-love, stay!'
    The constant Margaret cried;
Pale grew her cheeks, she closed her eyes,
    Stretched her soft limbs and died.

# YOUNG JOHN

A young girl sat at her cottage door,
  Wringing her lily-white hands;
She saw a sprightly youth run by
  Leaping over the land.

'Where are you going, young John?' she said,
  'So early in the day?
You run so fast it makes me think
  Your journey's far away.'

He turned on her with a surly look:
  And said, 'What's that to you?
I'm going to see a lovely girl,
  Far lovelier than you.'

'O, John, your love for me was once
  Like fields of summer flowers;
But now they're dead, and all that's left
  Is winter's stinging showers.

'But again, dear love, and again, dear love,
  Will you never love me again?
For if you look to other women,
  I'll look to other men.'

'Go and choose whoever you please,
  For I have made my choice;
I've chosen a girl that's fairer than you –
  She makes my heart rejoice.'

She fastened up her trailing skirt
  And after him ran she.
'Go back,' he said. 'Go back again!
  You shall not come with me.'

'But again, dear love, and again, dear love,
    Will you never love me again?
O, John, I've loved you far too well,
    Alas, I've loved in vain.'

When they came to the first town,
    He bought her brooch and ring,
Then begged her to turn back again
    And go no more with him.

When they came to the next town,
    He bought her shawl and gloves,
Then begged her to turn back again
    And choose some other loves.

'But again, dear love, and again, dear love,
    Will you never love me again?
O, John, I've loved you far too well,
    Alas, I've loved in vain.'

When they came to the next town,
    His heart grew warm within;
And he was as deep in love with her
    As ever she was with him.

When they came to the next town,
    He bought her a wedding gown,
And made her lady of every tower
    And hall in Berwick town.

## RIDDLE

In the dripping gloom I see
A creature with broad antlers,
Motionless. It turns its head;
One gleaming eye devours the dark.
I hear it cough and clear its throat;
Then, with a hungry roar,
it charges into the night
And is swallowed whole.

94

# GET UP AND SHUT THE DOOR

It happened one December night,
    And a dark night it was then,
That an old wife had puddings to make;
    She boiled them in the pan.

The wind blew cold from south and north,
    It blew across the floor;
The old man said to his old wife,
    'Get up and shut the door.'

'My hands are in the pudding basin,
    Husband, can't you see?
If it has to wait a hundred years,
    It won't be shut by me.'

They made a pact between the two,
    They made it firm and sure:
'The one who is the first to speak
    Gets up and shuts the door.'

Two gentlemen came passing by
    At twelve o'clock that night.
They couldn't see the house at all,
    Nor coal, nor candle-light.

They hit the house. 'May we come in?
    Is anyone there?' they cried.
And then they went in through the door,
    For no one had replied.

First they ate the white puddings,
    Then they ate the black;
But never a word the old wife spoke,
    Though she was hopping mad.

Then one man said to the other man,
    'Here now! Take my knife.
You cut off the old man's beard,
    And I will kiss his wife.'

'But there's no water in the house,
    So what shall we do then?'
'You'll have to use the pudding water
    Boiling in the pan.'

Then up sprang the old man,
    An angry man was he:
'What! Kiss my wife before my face
    And slop that muck on me?'

Then up sprang the old wife
    And gave three skips on the floor:
'Husband, you were the first to speak;
    Get up and shut the door.'

## THE CRAFTY FARMER

Farmer Jupp on a country road
    Was riding his dapple-grey,
When a highwayman caught up with him
    And courteously did say:

'Well met, well met! How far are you going?'
    Which made the farmer smile:
'Well met, if you're good company!
    I'm just going two mile.

'I rule no acres of my own,
    But hire a piece of ground.
I'm off to pay my landlord's rent –
    A thumping eighty pound.'

'Hush, hush!' replied the highwayman.
    'By east and west and south,
There may be robbers lurking here.
    You'd better shut your mouth.'

'The money's safe in my saddle-bag,'
    Said Jupp, 'And I'm on top.'
The stranger whipped his pistol out
    And, pointing it, cried, 'Stop!'

Jupp threw the saddle-bag over the hedge:
    'If you want it, sir, go find it!'
The thief slid off his horse to search,
    And told the farmer to mind it.

The farmer put his foot in the stirrup,
    And heaved his bulk astride;
To his landlord off he galloped, clapping
    Spurs to his horse's side.

'Come back!' called the highwayman. 'We'll share
    What's in your saddle-bag.'
He slashed the saddle with his sword
    And chopped it into rags.

From the stranger's saddle-bag the farmer
    Reaped ten times the rent;
Then paid the landlord twice his due,
    Which made him twice content.

When he came home, he shouted aloud,
    'Wife, you're rich as a duchess!'
And his old woman she capered for joy
    And danced him a jig on her crutches.

# THE RICH OLD LADY

A rich old lady in our town,
In our town did dwell;
She loved her husband dearly,
But another man twice as well.
       Sing Too de um! Sing Too de um!
       Whack! Fa lal a day!

She was listenin' in at the door one day,
When she heard the old man say
If you sniffed a few old marrow bones
It would take your sight away.
       Sing Too de um! etc.

So she went down to the butcher's shop
To see what she could find;
She wanted to buy a thing or two
To make her old man blind.
       Sing Too de um! etc.

She bought twelve dozen old marrow bones,
She made him sniff them all;
Says he, 'Old Lady, I now am blind,
I cannot see at all.
       Sing Too de um! etc.

'And I would like to drown myself
If I could only see –'
'Just take my hand, dear husband,
And come along with me.'
       Sing Too de um! etc.

She bundled him up in his old grey coat,
She led him to the brim.
Says he, 'I cannot drown myself
Unless – you push me in.'
      Sing Too de um! etc.

The old lady went up on the bank
To make a running dash;
The old man stepped a little to the side –
And in she went with a splash.
      Sing Too de um! etc.

She bubbled and gurgled and bawled out
As loud as she could squall.
Says he, 'Old lady, I'm *so* blind
I can't see you at all.'
      Sing Too de um! etc.

The old man being kind-hearted
And knowing she could not swim,
He went and cut him a very long pole
And – pushed her further in.
      Sing Too de um! etc.

WILLIE MACINTOSH

'Turn, Willie Macintosh,
   Turn, I tell you!
If you burn Auchindown,
   Huntly will kill you.'

Behead me or hang me,
    What do I care?
His castle shall burn,
    And I will be there.'

Coming down Deeside
    On a May morning,
The castle was blazing
    An hour before dawning.

'Brave Willie Macintosh,
    Where are your men?'
'Huntly rode after us,
    Caught us, and then –

'Look at them now!
    – O the heart-ache! –
They're asleep on the hill,
    And they will not wake.'

# THE BROWN GIRL

'I am as brown as brown can be,
  My eyes as black as a sloe;
I am as brisk as a nightingale,
  As wild as a woodland doe.

'My love has written a love-letter
  And sent it me from town;
He said he could not fancy me,
  Because my skin was brown.

'I sent his letter back again,
  For his love I valued not;
I cared not whether he fancied me
  Or whether he did not.

'He wrote that he was dangerous ill
  And begged me to go now
Most speedily, most speedily
  To free him from his vow.'

Now you shall hear what love she had
  For this poor love-sick man,
How all one day, a summer's day,
  She walked and never ran.

When she came to her love's bedside,
  Where he lay so ill and weak,
She laughed so much she could not stand
  Upright on her feet.

She took the rings from off her hands,
  By one, by two, by three:
'Take, O take these golden rings;
  By them remember me.'

She had a white wand in her hand
    And stroked it on his breast:
'Thus I free you from your vow;
    I hope your soul's at rest.'

'I beg you to forget,' he said,
    'Forget me and forgive;
O grant me a little longer time
    That I may be well and live!'

'You wish me to forget, forgive,
    But that I'll never do.
D'you think, because my skin is brown,
    I cannot feel as you?
I'll dance and sing on your green grave
    A year, a whole year through.'

## THE LYKE WAKE DIRGE

I sit and watch tonight, tonight,
    *Every night and all,*
By fire and hearth and candle-light;
    *And Christ receive your soul.*

When you have gone from here and passed,
    *Every night and all,*
To Whinny-moor you'll come at last;
    *And Christ receive your soul.*

If you have given shoes to the poor,
 *Every night and all,*
You'll walk unhurt on Whinny-moor;
 *And Christ receive your soul.*

If to the poor you've given none,
 *Every night and all,*
The gorse will prick you to the bone;
 *And Christ receive your soul.*

From Whinny-moor when you have passed,
 *Every night and all,*
You'll come to Bridge of Fear at last;
 *And Christ receive your soul.*

And when you pass from Bridge of Fear,
 *Every night and all,*
The fire of Hell will meet you here;
 *And Christ receive your soul.*

If you have given meat or drink,
 *Every night and all,*
The fire will never make you shrink;
 *And Christ receive your soul.*

If meat or drink you've given none,
 *Every night and all,*
The fire will burn you to the bone;
 *And Christ receive your soul.*

I sit and watch tonight, tonight,
 *Every night and all,*
By fire and hearth and candle-light;
 *And Christ receive your soul.*

# HOME CAME THE OLD MAN

1

O, home came the old man,
   And home came he,
And there he saw a strange horse
   Where his horse ought to be.

'My dear wife, my darling wife,
   What is this I see?
How did this horse come here
   Where my horse ought to be?'

'You stupid fool, you blind fool,
   Haven't you eyes to see?
It's nothing but a fat pig
   My mother sent to me.'

'A thousand miles I've ridden,
   A thousand miles I've been,
But a saddle on a pig's back
   I have never seen.'

2

O, home came the old man,
   And home came he,
And saw a pair of riding-boots
   Where his boots ought to be.

'My dear wife, my darling wife,
   What is this I see?
How did these boots come here
   Where my boots ought to be?'

'You stupid fool, you blind fool,
    Haven't you eyes to see?
It's nothing but two water-jugs
    Your mother sent to me.'

'A thousand miles I've ridden,
    A thousand miles I've been,
But silver spurs on water-jugs
    I have never seen.'

3

O, home came the old man,
    And home came he,
And there he saw a sword hung
    Where his sword ought to be.

'My dear wife, my darling wife,
    What is this I see?
How did this sword come here
    Where my sword ought to be?'

'You stupid fool, you blind fool,
    Haven't you eyes to see?
It's nothing but a walking stick
    My mother sent to me.'

'A thousand miles I've ridden,
    A thousand miles I've been,
But a walking stick of pointed steel
    I have never seen.'

**4**

O, home came the old man,
  And home came he,
And there he saw an overcoat
  Where his coat ought to be.

'My dear wife, my darling wife,
  What is this I see?
How did this coat come here
  Where my coat ought to be?'

'You stupid fool, you blind fool,
  Haven't you eyes to see?
It's nothing but a blanket
  My mother sent to me.'

'A thousand miles I've ridden,
  A thousand miles I've been,
But buttons on a blanket
  I have never seen.'

**5**

O, home came the old man,
  And home came he,
And there he saw a sturdy man
  Where no man ought to be.

'My dear wife, my darling wife,
  What is this I see?
How did this man come here
  Where no man ought to be?'

'You stupid fool, you blind fool,
  Haven't you eyes to see?
It's nothing but a servant girl
  My mother sent to me.'

'A thousand miles I've ridden,
    A thousand miles I've been,
But a servant girl with a brown beard
    I have never seen.'

6

He picked up his darling wife,
    Put her across his knee,
And gave her a beating then,
    One, two, three!

'My dear man, my darling man,
    What is this you do?'
'I'm giving you the kisses, dear,
    Your mother sent to you.'

# THE CRUEL MOTHER

I looked over the castle wall,
   *Hey rose, my lindy, O*
And saw two babies playing at ball.
   *Below the green wood side-y, O*

'O pretty babies, if you were mine,
I'd feed you with white bread and wine.'

'O cruel mother, we did not find,
When we were yours, you proved so kind.'

'O pretty babies, if you were mine,
I'd dress you both in scarlet fine.'

'O cruel mother, we did not find,
When we were yours, you proved so kind.

'You took a penknife, long and sharp,
And then you struck us to the heart.

'You lifted us and let us fall;
You threw us over the castle wall.'

'O pretty babies, what would you do
To a mother who'd been so cruel to you?'

'Seven years you'd be a fish in the sea,
Seven years you'd be a bird in the tree,

Seven years you'd be a tinkling bell,
Then seventeen years in deepest hell.'

'Welcome, welcome, fish in the sea,
Welcome, welcome, bird in the tree!

'Welcome, welcome, tinkling bell,
   *Hey rose, my lindy, O*
But heaven keep me out of hell!'
   *Below the green wood side-y, O.*

# THE LITTLE WEE MAN

As I was walking all alone
Between a river and a wall,
There I saw a little wee man –
I'd never seen a man so small.

His legs were barely a finger long,
His shoulders wide as fingers three;
Light and springing was his step,
And he stood lower than my knee.

He lifted a stone six feet high,
He lifted it up to his right knee,
Above his chest, above his head,
And flung it as far as I could see.

'O,' said I, 'how strong you are!
I wonder where your home can be.'
'Down the green valley there;
O will you come with me and see?'

So on we ran, and away we rode,
Until we came to his bonny home;
The roof was made of beaten gold,
The floor was made of crystal stone.

Pipers were playing, ladies dancing,
Four-and-twenty ladies gay;
And as they danced they were singing,
'Our little wee man's been long away.'

Out went the lights, on came the mist.
Where were the ladies? Where was he?
I looked and saw the wall and river . . .
That was all that I could see.

# INDEX OF TITLES

# INDEX OF FIRST LINES

# SOURCES

*Poems by Ian Serraillier*

Haiku: Alone I cling
Riddles:
   Cut me, and I'll make you cry
   I look at you
   White or grey
The Rescue
No Swimming in the Town
Jack
Spells:
   To be said to a balloon being blown up
   To get rid of the 'flu
   To find a lost season ticket
Prisoner and Judge
Riddles:
   What a hideous cackling and whistling
   These golden waves bow to the rule of the wind
Weeping Willow in my Garden
Not Sixteen
Fish in a Polluted River
The Will (based on a folktale told by Idries Shah in the programme
   'One Pair of Eyes' BBC2 TV)
Loudspeaker Song for a Supermarket
Jealousy
The Headless Gardener
Riddle:
   In the dripping gloom I see

*Adapted or slightly adapted from traditional ballads and songs*

Unless otherwise stated the originals all appear in *The English and
Scottish Popular Ballads* compiled by F. J. Child (Dover Publications,
New York, 1965), or in the abridged version of the book compiled by
H. C. Sargent and G. L. Kittredge (Houghton Mifflin Company, 1904
and 1932).

Waly, Waly (a Somerset folk-song which appears in the Elkin New
   Choral Series, edited by T. Armstrong)

Lord Thomas and Fair Annet
Lord Randal
Robin Hood and Alan-a-dale
The Hangman's Tree (this appears in the introduction to the Sargent
    and Kittredge version)
The Golden Vanity
Young Hunting
Little Musgrave
May Colvin
The Two Ravens (The Twa Corbies)
The Great Seal (The Great Silkie of Sule Skerry)
The False Knight upon the Road
The Gardener
The Unquiet Grave
Sweet William's Ghost
Young John (The False Lover Won Back)
Get Up and Shut the Door (Get Up and Bar the Door)
The Crafty Farmer
The Rich Old Lady (this appears in *American Folk Tales and Songs*,
    compiled by Richard Chase, New American Library, 1956)
Willie Macintosh
The Brown Girl
The Lyke Wake Dirge (this appears in the *Oxford Book of Ballads*)
Home Came the Old Man (Our Goodman)
The Cruel Mother
The Little Wee Man (The Wee Wee Man)


*Anon, with occasional changes of word*

Kiss Me Now (from *American Folk Tales and Songs*)
Lizzie Borden                            (these poems are taken from
As I was Coming Down the Stair  }  *Verse that is Fun* chosen by
The Centipede                            Barbara Ireson, Faber, 1962)
Limericks (unchanged)

# ANSWERS TO THE RIDDLES